The Black Dog

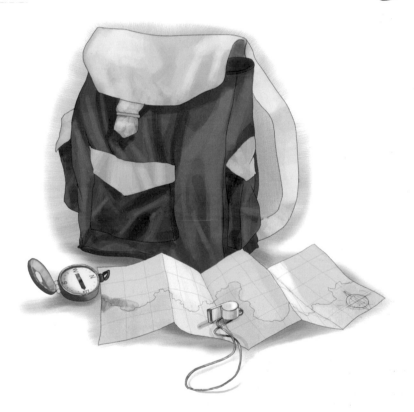

Written by Harriet Goodwin
Illustrated by Giorgio Bacchin

 Collins

Chapter 1

The children sat huddled around the campfire, nursing mugs of hot chocolate and watching as the flames danced before them and clouds of grey-blue smoke spiralled into the darkness.

"I'll just go and fetch those marshmallows," said Mr Middleton, getting up. "Then we'll have one more ghost story to round off the evening. I hope someone can think of a really spooky one to tell." He disappeared in the direction of his tent.

"I can't believe it's our last night here," sighed George. "This activity holiday's gone so fast."

Annie nodded. "It's been brilliant, hasn't it?"

"Brilliant for you, maybe," muttered a dark-haired boy sitting the other side of Annie. "Not so brilliant for me and George. You really messed up that challenge this afternoon, Annie. We'll never win the tournament now."

George rounded on him. "Oh, shut up Jed," he said. "She tried her best."

"Yeah," said Annie. "I did. I just didn't find the last part of the assault course very easy, that's all." She frowned at Jed. "Anyway, you haven't exactly been perfect yourself. Remember what happened on the first day? You couldn't get the hang of kayaking for ages. You kept drifting to one side of the river."

Jed scowled. "Yeah, that was because the stupid paddle kept getting stuck in the weeds. It wasn't like it was my fault."

Mr Middleton eyed them as he came back with the marshmallows.

"You three aren't arguing again, are you?" he said, shaking his head. "Honestly! None of the other teams has this problem." He sat down beside the fire and began sharing out the marshmallows.

"Looks like you lot are nearly ready for bed. Some of you are half asleep already. Who's going to tell the final story, then? Someone who hasn't had a turn yet? Jed? How about you?"

Jed shook his head. "I'm not really into spooky stories," he grunted. "I reckon they're for babies."

George laughed. "No they're not. And anyway, I've been watching you this evening. You've been just as freaked out as the rest of us."

Jed stared furiously at the ground as George turned to Mr Middleton. "I've got a story," he said. "It's one my dad told me. About a phantom black dog."

Twenty pairs of eyes looked at him.

"A phantom black dog?" said Mr Middleton. "That certainly sounds interesting." Leaning forwards, he tossed a large branch on to the fire. "All right then, George. Go on. We're all listening."

George dropped a marshmallow into the dregs of his hot chocolate and prodded it around with his spoon.

"Well," he started, lowering his voice so that the rest of the group had to crane forwards to hear him, "it happened nearly a hundred years ago, somewhere very close to here, actually. That's why my dad told me the story. My great-granddad was out walking in the woods, and he started to think he was being followed."

George spooned the marshmallow out of the bottom of his mug and chewed it slowly before going on.

"When he turned round, he couldn't see anything
except trees and shadows – but there was a strange
panting sound in the distance, and it seemed to be
getting closer. He remembered the old village legend,
about a phantom black dog. It was said that the hound
would pounce on anyone who dared walk over the place
where his master had died."

The children shifted uncomfortably around the fire.

"My granddad panicked," George went on. "He began to run through the woods, but it was almost dark by now and he couldn't find his way out. Suddenly the panting noise was right behind him, and he twisted round to see a huge black dog crouching in the shadows. It had a shaggy coat and rotten, stinking breath – and fire was dripping from its eyes."

"What – what happened next, George?" whispered Annie.

"The hound chased my great-granddad through the woods. All he could do was run and run until he was out the other side. Apparently his heart was beating so fast he thought it might explode inside him. When at last he looked behind him the dog had gone, but he never went into the woods again – and he was never quite the same after that day. The experience changed him forever."

There was an uneasy silence.

"I think it's a pathetic story," muttered Jed at last. "It'd take a lot more than a phantom hound to scare me."

George shrugged. "Whatever you say, Jed Towers," he said. "At least I had a story to tell."

Mr Middleton cleared his throat. "Well, I thought it was a great way to round off the evening," he said. "In fact I reckon this has been one of the best Campfire Nights I've ever known, and I've brought more groups to this place than I care to remember." He yawned. "And now it really is time for bed. It's our final day tomorrow and, trust me, you're going to need every wink of sleep you can get. I've got a hike planned for you in the morning."

The children groaned.

"And then it's back to camp for lunch before I set you your final challenge. So come on – into your tents, the lot of you. We'll wash up in the morning."

Everyone got to their feet, chattering and laughing as they made their way to their tents.

And in all the noise and fuss, no one noticed the howl coming from deep within the nearby woods.

Chapter 2

Mr Middleton unstrapped his rucksack and lowered it
on to the grass beside him.

"That was a great hike you managed this morning.
I don't think I heard a single complaint." He smiled at
the assembled group. "Anyway, I thought we should end
this activity holiday with a spot of orienteering.
Put your map and compass skills to the test and see
how well you've learnt to work within your teams.
So for your last challenge you'll be pleased to hear we're
going into the woods."

The children cheered.

"I'm going to take each team to a different location," Mr Middleton went on. "And when I blow my whistle your job is to use your maps and compasses to find your way out again. It's as simple as that. The first team back will win fifty points. Then I'll add up the final scores and see who's won the tournament."

Mr Middleton's expression grew more serious. "Needless to say, the usual teamwork rules apply. It's absolutely essential you stick together. No splintering off and going your own way, all right? I want you to think about everything we've learnt this week. About working in a group. About listening to one another. If you disagree about the direction you should take, then it's up to you to sort it out. I don't want to hear reports of any silly fighting."

His eyes flitted over the group of children, settling for a moment on Jed, who scowled and looked away.

"If you get lost just blow your whistle three times and I'll come in and get you – though obviously any team who needs my help won't be in with a chance of winning the points."

The children whispered excitedly amongst themselves while Mr Middleton began handing out pieces of equipment.

Jed turned to Annie and narrowed his eyes.

"You just keep out of things, OK?" he muttered. "Because this is one we *have* to win."

Chapter 3

"It's this way," said George. "It has to be." He stopped and spread the map out on the ground. "Look, according to the compass we're heading north-west. Which means we need to take this path here and …"

"You really think you know everything about orienteering, don't you?" cut in Jed. "If you'd just stop obsessing over that map and leave things to me we'd be out of here much quicker."

George wheeled round to face him.

"You mean we'd never be out of here," he retorted. "The whole reason we got lost in the first place is because you went rushing off before we'd had a chance to look at the map."

"Stop it, both of you!" said Annie. "Arguing isn't going to help." She stepped forwards. "Look, I've done this sort of thing before when I've been camping with my family. If you'd just let me look at the map, I might be able to work out where we are."

Jed laughed. "Yeah, right!" he scoffed. "In case you hadn't realised, we're actually trying to win this thing." He snatched the rucksack from Annie and stuffed the map and compass inside, not bothering to zip it up. "Let's just forget about the equipment. There's some light between the trees over there, and I bet that's where we need to be heading."

Slinging the rucksack over his shoulder, Jed darted off between the trees.

"Wait!" Annie called out after him. "Wait, Jed! One of my laces is undone."

But Jed wasn't listening. He stormed ahead through the nettles and brambles, and by the time the others were ready to follow, he was nowhere to be seen.

"What are we going to do now?"
said George, staring at Annie.
"He's disappeared – and he's taken the
rucksack with him. He's got the map.
The whistle. The compass. Everything."
He glanced up through the canopy
of trees. "It's very dark in here. D'you reckon
the sun's starting to go down already?"

"It can't be," replied Annie. "It's only
four o'clock. It's just the trees blocking out
the light." She sighed. "I wish Jed hadn't
gone off with the whistle. That was a pretty
stupid thing to do."

"A pretty *selfish* thing to do, you mean,"
said George. "Perhaps you should stay here
while I go after him. I reckon I can probably
find my way back to you."

Annie shook her head. "No way," she said.
"We've got to be sensible about this, George.
You heard what Mr Middleton said about
working as a team. We've got to go after
him together. We've got to ..."

She broke off as a howl echoed through
the forest.

"What was that?" whispered George. "Did you hear it?"

Annie bit her lip. "It was probably just Jed," she replied, trying to keep her voice from shaking. "He must have decided to play a joke on us. Spook us out after that story of yours last night."

"It didn't sound like Jed. It sounded like ..."

"George!" exclaimed Annie. "Just stop it, OK? If you carry on like this we'll never get out of here."

She picked up a fallen branch and began to beat a path through the already-flattened undergrowth.

"Come on," she said. "This is the way he went."

George glanced at her for a second, his face suddenly anxious and pale.

Then he followed her through the woods.

Chapter 4

Jed hurried on, muttering to himself under his breath. Where were the others? Why did they have to be so slow?

The light he thought he had sensed between the trees had turned out to be nothing more than a small clearing, and now he had got beyond it the woods seemed darker than ever.

He looked about him. A few minutes ago he'd heard voices in the distance: probably one of the other teams trying to find their way out. But now there was nothing. Well, he was hardly going to call out and admit he was lost, was he? After all the grief he'd given Annie, he'd never hear the end of it if he asked for help now.

A howl not far off had Jed skidding to a halt. His heart was hammering against his chest. What was that? Where had it come from? Was it one of the others playing a trick on him? Or could it be ...?

He steadied himself against a tree.

This was stupid. If it hadn't been for that story George had told last night he wouldn't be feeling like this. That was what was making him panic. That and the fact he was alone. He needed to take control of himself. He needed to get a grip.

Jed forced himself onwards ... but now he could hear another noise – a curious, rhythmic panting sound ...

Losing his footing, he lurched forwards and sprawled to the ground, cursing as the rucksack flew off his shoulder and landed in the undergrowth nearby.

He stumbled to his feet and glanced from side to side ... but he could see nothing. Only a haze of trees and nettles and brambles – and a familiar, suffocating darkness starting to pour towards him.

Jed reached out for the rucksack, trying to concentrate on his breathing.

In ... out ... in ... out ... Nice and steady. Just like he'd learnt to do when he had nightmares, when he woke drenched in sweat, his throat dry and his pulse racing.

And that was when he sensed it: something vast and dark lurking in the shadows behind him ...

Jed spun round, gripping the rucksack.

No more than a few feet away, its eyes glowing a fiery red, stood a huge black dog.

Chapter 5

"Still no sign of him," said Annie, pausing in the middle of a clearing and looking round at George. "This is ridiculous. D'you think he's found his way out already?"

George shrugged. "I guess it's possible," he replied. "But wouldn't Mr Middleton be in here looking for us by now if he'd done that? It wouldn't have taken him long to realise Jed had all the equipment and left us with nothing."

Annie considered for a moment. "Yes," she said. "You're right. He probably is still in here somewhere. We should just carry on looking."

"Don't you think we should call for help? One of the other teams might still be in the woods and if we shout loudly enough they might hear us."

"Go on, then," said Annie. "I suppose it wouldn't hurt to give it a go."

George cupped his hands to his mouth.

"Hello?" he called out. "Hello? Can anyone hear me?"

They strained their ears for a reply, but apart from the rustling of leaves and the occasional screech of a crow flying far above their heads, they couldn't hear anything.

George shouted out once more, but there was still no reply.

"It's not working," said Annie. "They must have all got out by now. Either that or we're way off-course and there's no one close enough to hear us."

Swallowing back the dryness in her throat, she pointed to the pathway of flattened nettles that started up beyond the clearing.

"Well, at least we know which way he went. I suppose we'll just have to carry on until we find him."

Chapter 6

Jed stood rooted to the spot.

It was vast. Bigger than any dog he'd ever seen. Its coat was dark and matted, its teeth yellow, its breath foul. Worst of all were its crimson eyes, which bored straight into his. There was no doubt about it. He was standing face to face with George's hound.

For a moment Jed's mind went blank and he could do nothing but gape at the beast in front of him.

And then his brain snapped into action.

The whistle! If he could just reach inside the rucksack and blow the whistle, then Mr Middleton would be with him straight away.

Hardly daring to breathe, Jed slid his hand into the open rucksack. He could feel the map, the little round compass, a slab of chocolate in one corner ...

His blood ran cold. The whistle wasn't there ...
It must have slipped out when he'd tripped over.

He glanced around the undergrowth for a flash of silver.

But now the massive hound was growling softly to itself and baring its teeth …

Jed staggered backwards.

It was too late for the whistle. Even if he could blow it right now, Mr Middleton wouldn't get to him in time. The only thing he could do was run.

He staggered backwards, crying out as his elbow jerked into a nearby tree.

The hound's fiery eyes widened. Its fur bristled and it drew back ready to pounce.

The next moment Jed was hurtling through the woods, the rucksack clutched to his chest.

Behind him he could hear the beast getting closer, its heavy panting mingling with the sound of his own jagged breaths, until it was no longer possible to tell the two noises apart …

Chapter 7

They heard him before they saw him. A rush of
thundering footsteps crashing towards them.

"Jed!" exclaimed Annie, as a figure burst out between
the trees. "Jed! What on earth's the matter?"

Jed fell against her, breathing heavily.
"It's coming after me!" he cried.
"The hound! The black dog! We've got to
get out of here ..."

Annie gaped at him. "Dog?"
she said. "What are you talking
about? I can't see any dog."

Jed glanced back the
way he had come,
wild-eyed.

"But it was
there!" he panted.
"I saw it. I swear I did.
It was chasing me through
the woods." His gaze flickered
over to George. "You know, one of
those things you were telling us about
last night."

George frowned. "It was a story, Jed.
Just a stupid story. You weren't supposed to
believe it or anything."

"I saw it!" said Jed. "It was exactly as you described.
A huge great beast. As big as a calf. It had stinking breath
and its eyes were glowing red ..." He broke off, shuddering
at the memory. "And I heard it, too. A howling noise
echoing through the woods. Didn't you?"

Annie and George glanced at one another.

"We did hear a noise," murmured George. "But – well, we thought it was probably just you messing about."

"It must have been one of the others," said Annie firmly. "After all, everyone heard George's story last night, didn't they? And it was pretty scary." She turned back to Jed. "I think you've had some sort of daytime nightmare."

Jed's face went crimson.

"Anyway," went on Annie, gesturing towards the rucksack. "I don't think we're going to win now, so let's just get on and blow the whistle."

"We can't," said Jed. "I haven't got it anymore."

"Haven't got it?"

"It must have fallen out of the rucksack. I tripped over and when I tried to find it, it wasn't there."

There was a very long silence.

"Well, there's only one thing to do then," said Annie. "We need to get out of here ourselves. Pass me the rucksack, will you? I want to look at the map."

"But ..."

"But what? Think I can't navigate our way out? Think I'm as hopeless at orienteering as I was at the assault course yesterday?" Annie grabbed the rucksack and pulled out the map and compass. "I told you, I've done this sort of thing before. I know what to do. You just wouldn't give me the chance to prove it."

The other two watched in silence as she turned the map this way and that, her eyes flitting over the tracks and pathways that snaked across the paper.

"Right then," she said at last. "I think I know where we are." She put on the rucksack and turned down a narrow track. "We're going to forget all about that dog, OK? We're going to concentrate on working together like we were supposed to do in the first place. And we're going to get ourselves out of these woods."

Chapter 8

This time the light in front of them was for real.
It grew stronger and stronger, until at last the trees
thinned out completely and they found themselves
standing on the edge of a familiar-looking field,
shielding their eyes from the late-afternoon sunlight
that streamed towards them.

"Look!" cried Annie. "There are all the others!
And Mr Middleton, too!" She pointed to where the
rest of the group were lying in the grass not far off,
basking in the sunshine.

"Looks like we're the last back, though," said George. "No chance of winning the tournament now."

Annie rolled her eyes at him. "Who cares?" she said. "We've got out of the woods – that's all that matters."

"Thanks to you," said Jed quietly. "Without you, we'd probably still be lost."

He turned to her. "I'm sorry I've given you such a hard time, Annie. I've been ..." He mumbled, the shadow of a smile curling round his lips. "I've been a complete nightmare."

Annie grinned at him. "Yes," she said. "You have. But I suppose I might just forgive you."

"Do you think you could possibly not say anything about all this?" asked Jed. "The rest of the group won't stop teasing me otherwise. Not in a million years."

Annie glanced at George. "What do you think?" she said. "We can keep this between ourselves, can't we?"

George gave her a sharp salute. "Whatever you say, boss!" he said. "It's fine by me! As far as I'm concerned it can be our little secret!"

Mr Middleton came hurrying across the field to greet them.

"I was just about to come and find you," he said. "I was starting to get a bit worried. The last team got out nearly ten minutes ago." He frowned. "Goodness me, Jed! Are you all right? You're completely covered in leaves and prickles. No strange sightings, I take it? No phantom black dogs roaming the woods?" He chuckled to himself.

"Of course not, Mr Middleton," replied Annie. "We just got a bit lost at one point, that's all. But it was nothing we couldn't handle." She winked at Jed and led the way down the field towards the others.

And behind them, hidden amongst the army of trees, the black shape that had followed them to the edge of the woods turned and disappeared into the shadows.

Mr Middleton's teamwork rules

1 don't argue

2 don't splinter off

3 stick together

Ideas for reading

Written by Linda Pagett B.Ed(hons), M.Ed
Lecturer and Educational Consultant

Learning objectives: reflect on how working in role helps to explore complex issues; explore how writers use language dramatic effects; use evidence from across a text to explain events or ideas; use a range of ICT programmes to present texts

Curriculum links: Citizenship

Interest words: assault course, campfire, compass, crimson, foul, jagged, kayaking, legend, matted, navigate, orienteering, pathetic, phantom, rucksack, scowled, suffocating, teamwork, tournament

Resources: collage materials, whiteboard

Getting started

This book can be read over two or more reading sessions.

- Invite the children to talk about times they've been frightened, and discuss how we feel when we're scared. Explain that the children are going to read a story that has fear as one of its themes.

- Encourage children to discuss times they have been away from home in a group, e.g. scout or guide camps, and the kind of ground rules involved. Discuss why these are important.

- Introduce the book by reading the blurb and encourage children to predict what the story may contain in light of the previous discussions.

Reading and responding

- Read pp2–5 together. Ask the children what themes the author has introduced, e.g. competitiveness, supporting others, taking responsibility for your own actions.

- Encourage children to read silently to the end of the chapter. Discuss the "story within a story" that George tells. How is he able to impart fear into his audience? What strategies does he use as a storyteller, e.g. pausing for effect at the bottom of p8?

- Encourage children to read to the end of the book. Listen to weaker readers throughout, prompting and praising where necessary.